Stuart

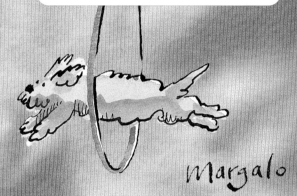

Margalo

Charlotte

Wilbur

Pook

# Puppies on Board

For Christian and Fiona
and in memory of Vera Nightingale Harvey.
*Omnia Vincit Amor* —S.N.H.

For my gorgeous girls, Georgia and Bailey;
my husband, Jeremy, who takes over when I need to get the job done;
and our "puppies," Josie and Jasper, who continually make us laugh. —R.C.

Text copyright © 2005 Sarah N. Harvey
Illustrations copyright © 2005 Rose Cowles

**National Library of Canada Cataloguing in Publication Data**
Harvey, Sarah N., 1950-

Puppies on board / story by Sarah N. Harvey; illustrations by Rose Cowles.

ISBN 1-55143-390-7

1. Puppies--Juvenile fiction. I. Cowles, Rose, 1967- II. Title.

PS8615.A766P86 2005          jC813'.6          C2005-902265-5

First published in the United States 2005
**Library of Congress Control Number:** 2005925305

**Summary**: When eleven puppies are born on her boat, Mollie must figure out how to find a home for each and every one.

Orca Book Publishers gratefully acknowledges the support for its publishing programs provided by the following agencies:
the Government of Canada through the Book Publishing Industry Development Program (BPIDP), the Canada Council for
the Arts, and the British Columbia Arts Council.

Design and typesetting by Lynn O'Rourke
Scanning by Island Graphics, Victoria, British Columbia
Artwork created using watercolors.

Orca Book Publishers          Orca Book Publishers
Box 5626 Stn. B              PO Box 468
Victoria, BC  Canada         Custer, WA   USA
V8R 6S4                      98240-0468

Printed and bound in Hong Kong
09 08 07 06 05 • 5 4 3 2 1

# PUPPIES
## ON BOARD

*story by* **Sarah N. Harvey**

*illustrations by* **Rose Cowles**

ORCA BOOK PUBLISHERS

What was that noise?

Mollie listened closely to the familiar sounds of morning on the wharf. Water lapped against the hull of the boat, halyards slapped against masts, rubber bumpers squeaked, seagulls squawked and boat engines roared, but the strange snuffly sound was still there.

It could only be one thing!

Mollie tiptoed past her sleeping mother and peeked into the wheelhouse. Sheba was in her pen, where they had left her the night before. But the night before she hadn't been licking and nuzzling a heap of damp, squirming puppies! At first Mollie could count only four or five, but as Sheba cleaned each one, Mollie counted six, then seven, then eight, nine and finally TEN wriggling, noisy, hungry puppies.

Then Mollie noticed something else—a tiny scrap of scraggly black fur tucked into the far corner of the pen. Ever so carefully, Mollie reached in and scooped up puppy number eleven. He was too small and weak to compete with his brothers and sisters, but he fit snugly into Mollie's cupped hands.

"I think I'll call you Wilbur," she whispered as she moved one of his greedy little brothers aside. "Eat your breakfast now, and don't worry—I'll look after you."

Every morning Mollie got up early to make sure that Wilbur was getting enough to eat. Every afternoon she took Sheba for a walk and helped her mother clean out the puppy pen, which seemed to get smaller and smellier as the puppies got bigger. Mollie's mother frowned as she stuffed a garbage bag with stinky newspaper.

"I wish your dad was here—he's a lot more patient than I am. One dog is enough for me."

Wilbur curled up with Mollie while she wrote to her dad, telling him all about the puppies.

Wilbur is trusting and loyal.
Charlotte is clever.

Heidi is curious.
Stuart is exuberant.

Margalo is beautiful.
Max is wild.

Pippi is adventurous.
Pooh is always hungry.

Piglet is timid.
Eeyore likes to hide.

And Tigger is very bouncy.

When the puppies were a few weeks old, they started climbing out of the wheelhouse, tumbling about the cockpit, chewing on boots and burrowing into bunks. Wilbur was too small to climb out of the pen, so Mollie carried him around in her backpack. You couldn't walk from the bow to the stern without stepping on a tiny tail. You couldn't eat without a puppy trying to share your meal, and you couldn't sleep without being woken up by little woofs and growls and squeaks.

Mollie's mother yawned as she drank her coffee in the morning sunshine with Sheba at her feet. She had just caught Max and Pippi scampering down the gangplank. The day before, Heidi had dived overboard and was rescued by Junichi, who lived with his father on their fishboat, the *Sazanami*. Wilbur followed Junichi down the wharf; Tigger and Piglet chewed up the charts; Eeyore hid in the bilge; and Stuart and Margalo jumped into a passing kayak for a cruise around the cove. Only Pooh and Charlotte were content to stay by Sheba's side.

"One dog is enough for me," sighed Mollie's mother, feeding Pooh a bit of her cinnamon bun. "I wish your father was here—he'd know how to find homes for them all."

"I have a plan," said Mollie.

Please come for tea
on the Brady Lee.
Saturday afternoon
at three.

From
Mollie and Wilbur

Mollie got out her felt pens and
some paper, and before long she had
made eight invitations, decorated
with her best stickers.

Early the next morning she set out
on her bicycle, with Wilbur and all
the invitations in the basket.

"What a sweet puppy," said Elizabeth, who lived in a little log cabin where she built guitars and grew prize-winning delphiniums. "I'd love to come for tea."

"What a goofy puppy," said Anne, who worked at the boatyard. "I'd love to come for tea."

"What a cute puppy," said Mollie's best friend Kelly, who lived in a big house filled with brothers and gumboots and the smell of freshly baked bread. "I'd love to come for tea."

"What a smart puppy," said Nina, who taught school with Mollie's mother. "I'd love to come for tea."

"What a cool puppy," said Alice and Kyle, who lived across the cove on a little green boat with their twin babies, Forest and Ocean.

"We'd love to come for tea."

"What a talented puppy," said Olaf, who played the saxophone in Mollie's father's band between fishing trips. "I'd love to come for tea."

"What a ridiculous puppy," said old Mrs. Morgan, who lived with only a parrot for company. "Maybe I'll come and maybe I won't. Will there be clotted cream?"

"I don't think so," said Mollie, "but it will be fun anyway."

Mollie rode back to the boat with only Wilbur and the last invitation in the basket. She walked down the wharf and slipped the invitation under a crab trap on the dock by the *Sazanami*.

On Saturday morning, Mollie and her mother made scones
and opened the blackberry jam they had made last summer.
Max climbed in the flour bin and started to sneeze. Stuart
and Margalo made an awful ruckus with the pots and pans,
and Mollie's mother groaned when Tigger climbed onto the
counter and ate three scones. Mollie scooped up the puppies
and calmed them down with puppy treats and a story. When
they were all asleep, she sat down on the afterdeck of the
*Brady Lee* to see if her plan would work.

Elizabeth arrived first with a big bouquet of delphiniums and a guitar. Alice, Kyle and the twins came next with Olaf, who brought his saxophone.

Kelly brought her mother and a big loaf of banana bread, and Nina arrived with Anne and a basket of ripe strawberries. Mrs. Morgan turned up with a crock of clotted cream and an old umbrella to keep off the sun. Junichi and his father sat on the wharf because there was no more room on the *Brady Lee*.

Mollie and her mother served three kinds of tea—chamomile, Earl Grey and green—and everyone remarked on the fluffiness of the scones, the richness of the cream, the sweetness of the strawberries and the lusciousness of the jam. Mollie wished her dad were there, getting cream in his beard and making her mother giggle.

After tea was finished, Elizabeth and Olaf played duets, Forest and Ocean gurgled, and a couple of the puppies howled along with the music.

"Those are mighty talented puppies," said Olaf, picking up Charlotte and Tigger. "Can I take them fishing with me?"

"Sure," said Mollie, "but don't let them fall overboard."

"These two belong together," said Elizabeth, cradling Pooh and Piglet in her arms. "Can I take them home and write songs about them?"

"Absolutely," said Mollie, "but don't let them dig up the delphiniums."

"These little clowns make me laugh," said Anne, juggling Max and Pippi. "Can I take them back to the boatyard to keep me company?"

"Certainly," said Mollie, "but don't let them stow away on one of the boats."

"Please, Mom," said Kelly, hugging Heidi to her chest, "I've only got brothers and this one's so cute. Can I take her home?"

"All right," said Kelly's mom, "if it's okay with Mollie."

"It's perfectly okay," said Mollie, "but don't dress her up in doll clothes."

"Hmmm," said Nina, examining Margalo from every angle. "I think she's as intelligent as she is beautiful. Can I take her home and teach her tricks?"

"Please do," said Mollie, "but don't make her work too hard."

Eeyore was snuggled between Forest and Ocean.

"He'll keep the babies warm on cold nights. Can we take him exploring?" asked Alice.

"Yup," said Mollie, "but don't let him wander off alone."

"Well," said Mrs. Morgan, "this is ridiculous, but I'm tired of talking to the parrot. Hand me the last two—they can keep each other company."

"Well," said Mollie slowly, "you can have Stuart, if you don't let him get too carried away, but you can't have Wilbur."

"Oh!" said Mrs. Morgan.

"Oh?" said Mollie's mother. "You know one dog is enough for me, Mollie."

"I know," said Mollie as she jumped off the boat, "but I have a feeling that one dog will be just right for Junichi, too."

"*Arigato*, Mollie," said Junichi's dad, with a bow.

"You're welcome," said Mollie, "but don't take him too far away."

"I won't," said Junichi as he and Wilbur hopped aboard the *Brady Lee*.